This book belongs to:

_____

to
Martha, Pepa,
Daphne and Maia

First published in Great Britain in 2006 by Andersen Press Ltd., 20 Vauxhall Bridge Road, London SW1V 2SA.
This paperback edition first published in 2007 by Andersen Press Ltd.
Published in Australia by Random House Australia Pty., Level 3, 100 Pacific Highway, North Sydney, NSW 2060.
Copyright © David Lucas, 2006
The rights of David Lucas to be identified as the author and illustrator
of this work have been asserted by him in accordance with the Copyright, Designs and Patents Act, 1988.
All rights reserved. Colour separated in Italy by Beverari, Verona.
Printed and bound in Singapore.

10   9   8   7   6   5   4   3   2   1

British Library Cataloguing in Publication Data available.

ISBN 978 1 84270 608 4

This book has been printed on acid-free paper

whale

David Lucas

Andersen Press • London

Joe was sound asleep,
as the waves crashed on the shore
and the windows rattled in the gale.
Until *barooom!*
the whole house shook,
the floor tipped up, and
Joe fell out of bed.

It was morning, but it was still dark outside.
Something was wrong.

"Grandma May," said Joe.
"It's still dark outside!"
They went to the door…
but they couldn't get out.

Joe ran up to the attic.
"There's someone at the window!"

Grandma May put on
her Going Out Hat
and grabbed her umbrella.
"Right, come on then," she said.
"Up the chimney!"

They stood on the roof.
"A fish!"
said Grandma May.
"A *whale*,"
said Joe in awe.

Joe and Grandma May clambered up…up…up to the top of the Whale. There, the townsfolk were all talking at once, and there was the Owl that had lived in the Clock Tower. The Mayor spoke up:

"O Whale! What have you done? Our town is ruined."

"I'm truly sorry," boomed the Whale.

"I was frolicking in the bay, singing in the storm. I got carried away trying to balance on my tail. Now I'm done for. You may as well chop me in pieces. I would make a magnificent fish pie."

"He would indeed," agreed the Fishmonger.

"But we *must* help the Whale!" said Joe.
"How?" asked the Mayor.
"I don't know," said Joe.

"At least let me ask the Owl," said Joe.
"*Hoo* now," said the Owl. "Let me ask the Wind,"
and the Owl flew high in the air.
"He really would make a magnificent fish pie,"
said the Fishmonger.
"No!" said Joe.

At last the Owl returned.

"I have spoken to the Wind," he said.

"The Wind has gone to speak to the Sun.

The Sun will want to speak to the Moon.

The Moon will want to speak to the Innumerable Stars.

The Innumerable Stars will, no doubt, want to talk it over

amongst themselves."

"Then we must wait," said Joe.

And so they waited…

…and waited.

It was morning when at last the Wind fluttered in the Owl's ear.

"The Wind has spoken to the Sun," said the Owl.

"The Sun has spoken to the Moon,
the Moon has spoken to the Innumerable Stars,
the Innumerable Stars have talked amongst themselves,
and they are all agreed that we must sing."

"Sing?" said the Mayor.

"Sing?" said the Fishmonger.

"But what shall we sing?" asked Grandma May.

"The Rain Song!" suggested Joe.

"The Rain Song doesn't work," said the Mayor.
"Everyone knows that."
But Joe began to sing, the Owl began to hoot,
Grandma May began to sing.
They all began to sing:
"Rain rain, splish splash,
Thunder crack and lightning flash!"
And then the Whale joined in,
in a voice so big the land shook.

It was only a song.
They hadn't really
expected it to work…

Soon the whole town was flooded.
The Whale was afloat.
"But now *we* are stuck!" said the Mayor.

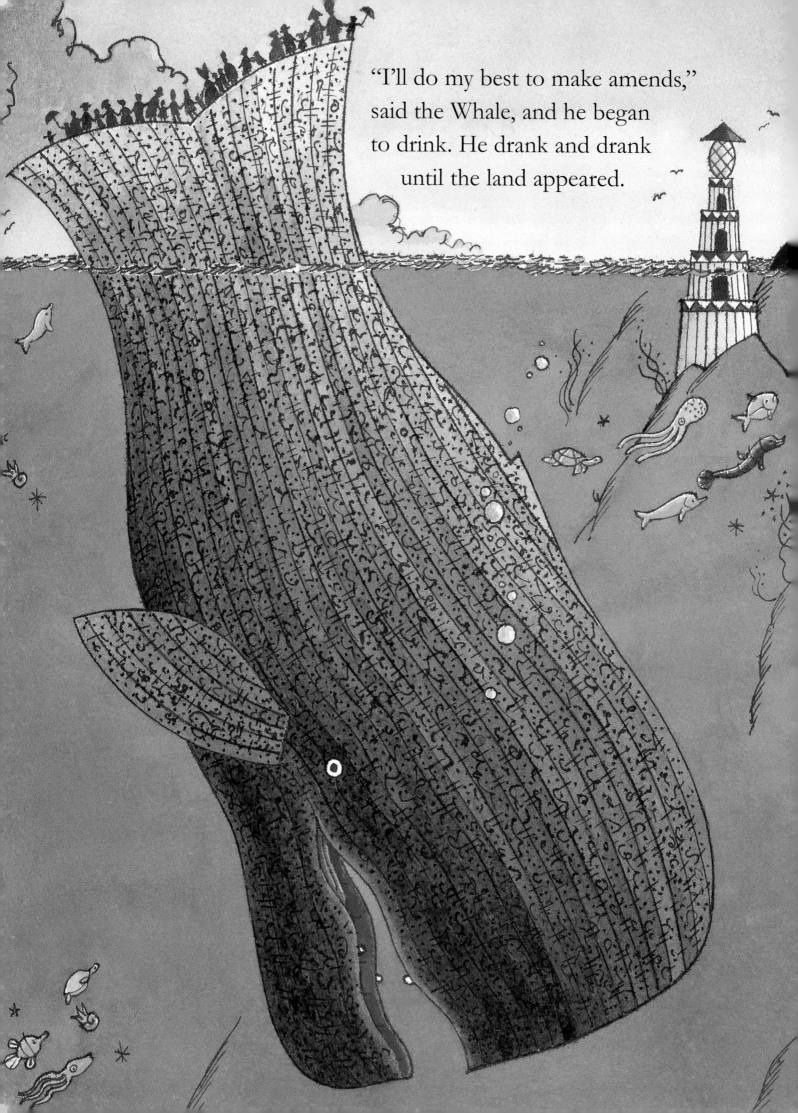

"I'll do my best to make amends," said the Whale, and he began to drink. He drank and drank until the land appeared.

And one by one, the
townsfolk went ashore.
"Our town!"
groaned the Mayor.
"Oh dear!" said Joe.

But out in the bay the Whale was singing.
"It's fish language," the Owl whispered to Joe.
And every kind of sea creature came swimming towards the shore,
carrying shells and bright pebbles and pearls.
And an army of fiddler crabs marched up the beach
and set about making the town more beautiful than ever before.

The townsfolk were delighted.

"Thank you, Whale!" they said, and waved goodbye.

"Goodbye!" boomed the Whale. "Thank you, Joe," he called.

"I promise I'll come back and see you again one day!"

other books by
DAVID LUCAS

'Instant classic for once really
does spring to mind'
FINANCIAL TIMES

'A lovely, sparky story'
OBSERVER

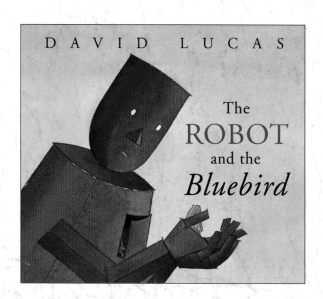